D0852218

THE
little
french
whistle

by Carole Lexa Schaefer
illustrated by Emilie Chollat

Alfred A. Knopf
New York

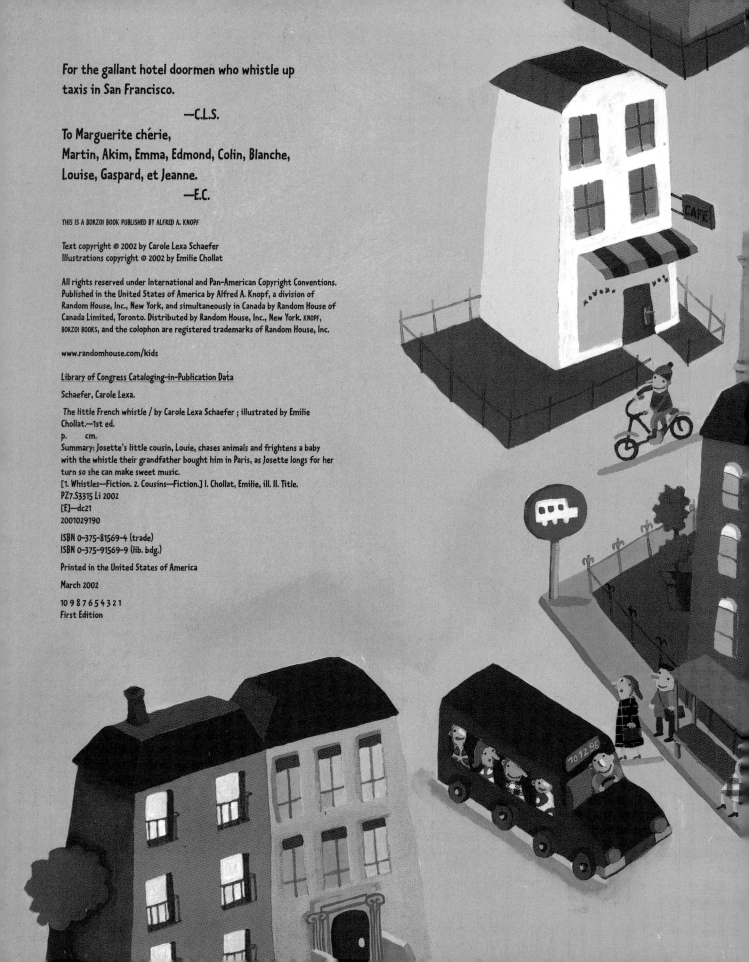

For the gallant hotel doormen who whistle up
taxis in San Francisco.

—C.L.S.

To Marguerite chérie,
Martin, Akim, Emma, Edmond, Colin, Blanche,
Louise, Gaspard, et Jeanne.

—E.C.

THIS IS A BORZOI BOOK PUBLISHED BY ALFRED A. KNOPF

Text copyright © 2002 by Carole Lexa Schaefer
Illustrations copyright © 2002 by Emilie Chollat

www.randomhouse.com/kids

Library of Congress Cataloging-in-Publication Data
Schaefer, Carole Lexa.
 The little French whistle / by Carole Lexa Schaefer ; illustrated by Emilie
Chollat.—1st ed.
 p.   cm.
Summary: Josette's little cousin, Louie, chases animals and frightens a baby
with the whistle their grandfather bought him in Paris, as Josette longs for her
turn so she can make sweet music.
[1. Whistles—Fiction. 2. Cousins—Fiction.] I. Chollat, Emilie, ill. II. Title.
PZ7.S3315 Li 2002
[E]—dc21
2001029190

ISBN 0-375-81569-4 (trade)
ISBN 0-375-91569-9 (lib. bdg.)

Printed in the United States of America

March 2002

10 9 8 7 6 5 4 3 2 1
First Edition

This morning
Auntie Claire and
my little cousin, Louie,
came to visit at our house.

Mama says Louie is spoiled. I say he is just Louie.

Louie brought along his little French whistle. Grand-père bought it for him in Paris, across the sea.

Louie blew his whistle.

WHOUi!
WHOUi!
WHOUi!

It sounded important and snappy to me. I, Josette, wanted to try it.

"Louie," I said, "may I blow your whistle?"
Louie stomped his foot. *"Non!"* he said in French, like Grand-père.

I still wanted a turn with the whistle. So I followed Louie to see what would happen.

In our small garden, Louie blew at
the birds in the gurgling birdbath.

They all flew away.

"If you played it sweet, *mon cher*,"
said Auntie Claire, "those birdies
might sing for you."

"*Non!*" said Louie. "I don't *like* sweet."

"Maybe not," I said. "But your whistle might."

Louie paid no attention to me.
Instead, he snuck up on Fonfon,
our dog, who was snoozing.

Fonfon jumped up and yip-yapped away.

"Louie," said Mama, "can't you blow *soft* on that whistle?"
"*Non!*" said Louie. "I don't *like* soft."
"But I bet it's something your whistle can do," I said.

Louie did not listen. He marched upstairs...

...and into the bathroom, where Grand-père was taking a bubble bath.
Louie blew right into the bubbles.

"*Zut, alors!*" cried Grand-père. "Do you want me to send that whistle back to Paree?"

"*Non!*" said Louie. "I don't *like* Paree."

"But Louie," I said, "in Paree, they make whistle music all day long. Want me to show you how?"

"*Non!*" said Louie. "*Non!*" He strutted downstairs...

...and out our front door.

On the sidewalk, Nanny Susan from next door wheeled baby Roland in his stroller.

Louie blew as sharp as Grand-père
whistling for a taxi to stop at our curb.

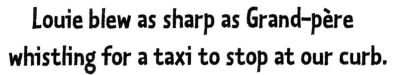

**WHOUI !
WHOUI !
WHOUI !**

It sounded grand to me,
but baby Roland cried.

Louie skittered
back into our house.

In the parlor on the puffy purple chair sat Sheba,
our cat, cleaning one of her big front paws.
Louie snuck up next to her.

He blew so hard that Sheba's whiskers quivered.

Sheba swatted at Louie and the little French whistle.

Up it flew.
And down it came.

But Louie didn't see where because
Sheba stood glaring and hissing at him.

"I can help you find your whistle, Louie," I said.
"Non!" he shouted. "I want to go home."
So Auntie Claire took Louie home, *without* his whistle.

But I knew he'd be mad and sad later and want it
back again. That was just Louie. So I slid my hand way
down in the creases of the puffy purple chair . . .

. . . and pulled out the little French whistle.

Then, since I, Josette, had found it, I took my turn.
I blew it sweet for the birds:

They twittered back:

I whistled it soft for Fonfon:

He came dancing to me on his short little legs.

I played it soft *and* sweet for Sheba:

R-r-r, she purred. *R-r-r.*

I warbled on it for Grand-père, who was on his way out to Louie's house for tea.

"*Voilà*, Josette," said Grand-père. "You make music like in Paree."

I followed him to the sidewalk and blew the little French whistle one more time.

I blew it like Louie—important, and snappy, and grand.

And...

A taxi stopped right at our front curb.
Grand-père got in—*mais oui.*
Along with...

...the little French whistle, and me.